This book belongs to

....

....

....

For Grace and Samuel – M. M.

Dedicated to the memory of Mattie Murray, a wonderful mum.

And to all mums everywhere – A. M.

ORCHARD BOOKS

First published in Great Britain in 2018 by The Watts Publishing Group

Texts for *Speckledy Hen Bakes a Cake, Twenty Cheeky Monkeys, Little Peachling and the Giants, Three Magic Wishes, Anna and the Shaggy Bear* and *The Little Red Hen and the Rascally Fox* previously published in Great Britain in 1999 as part of *Sleepytime Stories*; texts for *Goldilocks and the Three Bears, The Ugly Duckling, The Three Little Pigs, The Enormous Turnip, The Town Mouse and the Country Mouse* and *The Elves and the Shoemaker* previously published in Great Britain in 1991 as part of *The Orchard Book of Nursery Stories*

1 3 5 7 9 10 8 6 4 2

Texts for *Speckledy Hen Bakes a Cake, Twenty Cheeky Monkeys, Little Peachling and the Giants, Three Magic Wishes, Anna and the Shaggy Bear* and *The Little Red Hen and the Rascally Fox* © Margaret Mayo, 1999, 2018

Texts for *Goldilocks and the Three Bears, The Ugly Duckling, The Three Little Pigs, The Enormous Turnip, The Town Mouse and the Country Mouse* and *The Elves and the Shoemaker* © Hachette Children's Group, 1991, 2018

Illustrations © Alison Murray, 2018

A CIP catalogue record for this book is available from the British Library.

ISBN 978 1 40835 078 2

Printed and bound in China

Orchard Books
An imprint of Hachette Children's Group
Part of The Watts Publishing Group Limited
Carmelite House, 50 Victoria Embankment, London EC4Y 0DZ

An Hachette UK Company
www.hachette.co.uk

www.hachettechildrens.co.uk

MIX
Paper from responsible sources
FSC® C104740
FSC
www.fsc.org

ORCHARD

Bedtime Stories

With stories by
MARGARET MAYO

Illustrated by
ALISON MURRAY

ORCHARD

Contents

Goldilocks
and the Three Bears

ONCE UPON A TIME, there were three bears who lived in a little cottage deep in the woods. There was a great big Father Bear, a middle-sized Mother Bear and a tiny wee Baby Bear.

Father Bear had a great big bowl to eat from, a great big chair to sit on, and a great big bed to sleep in.

Mother Bear had a middle-sized bowl to eat from, a middle-sized chair to sit on, and a middle-sized bed to sleep in. And Baby Bear had a tiny wee bowl to eat from, a tiny wee chair to sit on, and a tiny wee bed to sleep in, all for himself.

One day, Mother Bear cooked some porridge for breakfast and ladled it into their three bowls. The porridge was far too hot to eat, so the three bears went for a walk in the woods while they waited for it to cool.

The three bears had not been gone long when a

little girl came by. She had wandered into the woods to pick flowers and was far from home. Her name was Goldilocks.

Goldilocks was tired and hungry after her long walk, so she was happy to see the three bears' cottage. She knocked on the door. There was no reply, but the door swung open and she went inside.

On the kitchen table, Goldilocks saw the three bowls of porridge. How hungry she was!

First she tasted the porridge in the great big bowl. "Too hot!" said Goldilocks.

Next she tasted the porridge in the medium-sized bowl. "Too cold!" said Goldilocks.

Finally she tasted the porridge in the tiny wee bowl. "Mmm, just right!" she said and ate it all up.

Then Goldilocks saw the bears' three chairs, and decided to sit down and rest.

First she sat on the great big chair. "Too hard." Next she sat on the middle-sized chair. "Too soft." Then she sat on the tiny wee chair. "Just right," said Goldilocks.

But all of a sudden – *crack!* – the chair broke into pieces and down fell Goldilocks – *crash!* – on to the floor.

Now Goldilocks felt quite sleepy, so up the stairs she went to find the bedroom.

First she lay down on the great big bed. "Too hard." Next she lay down on the middle-sized bed. "Too soft." Then she lay down on the tiny wee bed. "Just right," said Goldilocks and she fell asleep at once.

While Goldilocks was sleeping, the three bears came back from their walk in the woods. They went straight to their bowls of porridge, waiting on the kitchen table.

"Who's been eating my porridge?" said Father Bear in his rough, gruff voice.

"Who's been eating my porridge?" said Mother Bear in her soft voice.

"Who's been eating my porridge?" said Baby Bear in his tiny wee voice. "It's *all gone*!"

Then the three bears looked at their chairs.

"Who's been sitting on my chair?" said Father Bear in his rough, gruff voice.

"Who's been sitting on my chair?" said Mother Bear in her soft voice.

"Who's been sitting on my chair and broken it all to bits?" said Baby Bear in his tiny wee voice, and he started to cry.

Next the three bears went upstairs to the bedroom.

"Who's been sleeping in my bed?" said Father Bear in his rough, gruff voice.

"Who's been sleeping in my bed?" said Mother Bear in her soft voice.

"Who's sleeping in my bed? She's still there!" said Baby Bear in his tiny wee voice.

Of course, Goldilocks woke at once. She jumped from the bed, ran down the stairs, and hurried out of the door and away into the woods.

And that was the last the three bears ever saw of Goldilocks.

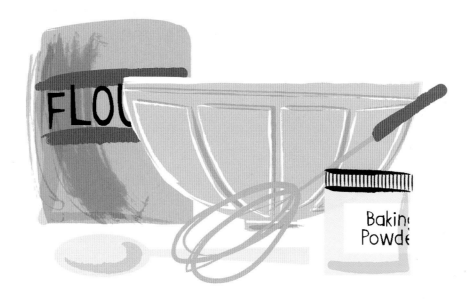

Speckledy Hen
Bakes a Cake

SPECKLEDY HEN and her five fluffy chicks lived in a little house with Spotted Dog, Ginger Cat and Pink Pig. Speckledy Hen always did all the work, while Spotted Dog, Ginger Cat and Pink Pig did none.

One day Speckledy Hen decided to bake a cake, and she said, "Now who will help me mix the cake?"

"I won't," said Spotted Dog. "I want to play with my bone."

"I won't," said Ginger Cat. "I want to play with my ball."

"And I won't," said Pink Pig. "I want to roll in the grass."

"Then I'll do it myself!" said Speckledy Hen.

So she mixed the butter, sugar, eggs and flour, and her five fluffy chicks gathered round and they tried to help. *Cheep! cheep! cheep!*

When the mixture was ready, Speckledy Hen called, "Now who will help me cook the cake?"

"I won't," said Spotted Dog. "I want to go for a run."

SPECKLEDY HEN BAKES A CAKE

"I won't," said Ginger Cat. "I want to climb a tree."

"And I won't," said Pink Pig. "I want to go for a walk."

"Then I'll do it myself!" said Speckledy Hen.

And she poured the mixture into a tin, popped the tin in the hot oven, and her five fluffy chicks gathered round, and they tried to help. *Cheep! cheep! cheep!*

When the cake was golden-brown and ready, Speckledy Hen took it out

of the oven and she called, "Now who will help me set the table?"

"I won't," said Spotted Dog. "I'm tired, and I want to sleep."

"I won't," said Ginger Cat. "I'm tired, and I want to sleep."

"And I won't," said Pink Pig. "I'm tired too, and I want to sleep."

"Then I'll do it myself!" said Speckledy Hen.

And she did, and her five fluffy chicks tried to help. *Cheep! cheep! cheep!*

"Now," said Speckledy Hen, "who will help me EAT the cake?"

"I will!" cried Spotted Dog, jumping up and wagging his tail.

"I will!" cried Ginger Cat, jumping up and licking her lips.

"And I will!" cried Pink Pig, jumping up and grunting.

"Oh no, you won't!" said Speckledy Hen. And she called her five fluffy chicks. Then Speckledy Hen and her five fluffy chicks ate all the cake . . . every last crumb.

The Ugly Duckling

ONCE UPON A TIME, there was a mother duck who lived beside a lake with her nine ducklings. Eight of them were pretty, fluffy, yellow ducklings, but the ninth one was a dirty grey colour, with a long, thin neck.

"What an ugly little duckling you are!" his mother would say to him. And his brothers and sisters would tease him and peck him and try to chase him away.

"You don't belong in our family, you're too ugly!" they said to the ugly duckling. "Go away! We don't want you here."

So the ugly duckling stayed away from his brothers and sisters. Whenever their mother took them walking along the shore, or taught them to swim on the lake, he was careful to stay at the back, out of sight. He was very unhappy indeed.

Now, as soon as her ducklings could swim well enough, the mother duck took them across the lake to visit their cousins.

She set off over the water with her ducklings swimming in a long line behind her. The ugly duckling swam at the back as usual. He was the last to waddle out of the water, trying his hardest to keep out of sight of the other ducks.

But it was no good. His cousins noticed him immediately. "What's this ugly creature?" said one of the drakes, giving him a sharp poke.

"You can't be a duck," said another.

All the ducks were shouting and pointing.

The ugly duckling was so unhappy that he ran away and hid in the reeds. "I *am* a duck! I *am*!" he sobbed.

Soon it grew dark. The ugly duckling couldn't see his mother or his brothers and sisters. He wandered about in the reeds, unable to find his way home. Then, feeling very small and lonely, he curled up and went to sleep.

The next morning, as the ugly duckling dabbled around in the water, looking for food, two wild ducks flew down. "What kind of bird are you?" asked one.

"I'm a duck," said the ugly duckling.

"Funny kind of duck!" said one wild duck to the other.

Off waddled the ugly duckling, away from the wild

ducks, stumbling through marshes and meadows, until he came to another lake. He found long reeds to hide in and plenty of food. *No one will find me here,* he thought.

Days became weeks. The ugly duckling stayed by the lake. The nights grew darker and a cold wind blew from the north.

Then one day the ugly duckling saw some swans flying south for the winter. How beautiful they were, with their great white wings beating slowly through the sky.

"Why don't you come with us?" they called to him.

"Wait for me! I'm coming!" cried the ugly duckling. He flapped his wings, but they weren't yet strong enough to fly. He couldn't take off and the swans were soon far away.

Eventually summer came. The ugly duckling felt the sun, warm on his neck. He stretched out his wings, which were big and strong by now. Then – with a mighty flap – he took off into the air.

"I'm flying! I'm really flying!"

He soared through the sky, over fields and hills, till he came to a river. A flock of graceful swans was gliding along it, their long necks proudly arched.

"Come and join us," called the swans.

"Who, me?" cried the ugly duckling. "You don't want me! I'm only an ugly duckling."

"A duckling? Why, you're a swan just like us. Look at yourself!"

The ugly duckling peered into the water. Staring back at him was a graceful, white-feathered swan. He was no longer clumsy. No longer grey and ugly. He was beautiful! The other swans gathered around him and together they swam off downstream. And the ugly duckling who had become a swan lived happily ever after.

The Three
Little Pigs

ONCE UPON A TIME, there were three little pigs who left their home and their parents and went out into the world to seek their fortune.

The first little pig set off through the fields. It wasn't very long before he met a man who was carrying a bundle of straw.

"Please, Man," said the little pig, "will you give me

some straw so I can build myself a house?"

"As much as you need, Little Pig," said the man.

He gave the straw to the little pig, and the little pig built himself a straw house.

In a little while, a wolf came knocking on the door.

"Little Pig, Little Pig," said the wolf, "let me come in."

"No, no, by the hair of my chinny chin chin, I will not let you in," said the little pig.

"Then I'll huff and I'll puff and I'll blow your house down," said the wolf.

And he huffed and he puffed and he blew the straw house down and ate up the first little pig.

The second little pig went up the hill to the woods. There he met a man who was carrying a bundle of sticks.

"Please, Man," said the little pig, "will you give me some sticks so I can build myself a house?"

"As many as you need, Little Pig," said the man.

He gave some sticks to the little pig, and the little pig built himself a wooden house.

Soon the wolf came knocking on the door.

"Little Pig, Little Pig," said the wolf, "let me come in."

"No, no, by the hair of my chinny chin chin, I will not let you in," said the little pig.

"Then I'll huff and I'll puff and I'll blow your house down," snarled the wolf.

And he huffed and he puffed and he blew the wooden house down and ate up the second little pig.

The third little pig skipped down the lane to the town. On the way, she met a man carrying a load of bricks.

"Please, Man," said the little pig, "will you give me some bricks so I can build myself a house?"

"As many as you need, Little Pig," said the man.

He gave some bricks to the little pig, and the little pig built herself a brick house.

No sooner had the little pig settled into her new home than the wolf came knocking.

"Little Pig, Little Pig," said the wolf, "let me come in."

"No, no, by the hair of my chinny chin chin, I will not let you in," said the little pig.

"Then I'll huff and I'll puff and I'll blow your house down," roared the wolf.

And he huffed and he puffed, and he huffed and he puffed, but he couldn't blow down the strong brick house.

The wolf was angry. He sprang up on to the roof and shouted, "Little Pig, I'm coming down the chimney!"

THE THREE LITTLE PIGS

But the little pig was ready for the wolf. She had a big pot of water boiling on the fire, and when she lifted the lid, the wolf fell right into the pot. The little pig slammed the lid on the pot, and that was the end of the wicked wolf.

And the little pig lived safe and snug in her little brick house for the rest of her life.

Three
Magic Wishes

JACK WAS A POOR WOODCUTTER who lived with his wife, Mary, in a little log hut beside a forest.

One day, when he was deep in the forest, cutting down trees, he saw a big old tree he hadn't noticed before.

"That's a fine tree," he said. "I'll cut it down."

He swung his axe over his shoulder and was just going to wham it down when a small, soft voice called,

"Stop, Mr Woodcutter! Don't cut down this tree!"

Then Jack saw, way up in the branches, a teeny tiny man. He was dressed in green, except for his pointy brown slippers, while in his hands he held a pointy red hat. The teeny tiny man was a woodland elf.

"I wouldn't chop down your house, Mr Woodcutter," said the elf. "So, please, don't chop down mine. This big tree is where I live."

Jack frowned and scratched his head. "*Whoo!* If you live here," he said, "of course I won't chop the tree down!"

"Then you shall have a thank-you present," said the elf. "You shall have three magic wishes. But, Mr Woodcutter, be careful how you use them!"

With that, the elf stuck the pointy red hat firmly on his head and was gone. Maybe you have guessed – it was a magic hat, and when the elf put it on, nobody could see him.

When Jack got home to his little hut that evening, he was very hungry, and the first thing he said was, "What's for supper, Mary?"

"Cabbage soup," she said.

"Not cabbage soup again!" grumbled Jack. "I wish I had a big fat sausage!"

And – *pfff!* – a frying pan, with a sausage in it going *sizzle-sizzle!* came flying through the air, and landed on the stove.

"Oh! That's one wish gone!" said Jack. "I quite forgot." And then he told Mary about the elf and the three magic wishes.

"Three magic wishes, and you wasted one on a SAUSAGE!" cried Mary. "You could have wished for a new house, or some money. I am so cross, I wish . . . *I wish that sausage was stuck on your nose!*"

And – *pfff!* – the sausage jumped up and stuck itself on the end of Jack's nose.

"Oh! That's two wishes gone!" said Jack. "Now what shall we do? I can't go round with a big fat sausage stuck on my nose!"

"I'll pull it off," said Mary. And she grabbed the sausage and pulled. But it was stuck fast on his nose. She couldn't move it.

"I'll cut it off," said Mary.

"No! You might cut off my nose," cried Jack. "There is only one thing we can do. I'll have to use the last wish."

"Oh, no!" cried Mary.

"Oh, yes!" said Jack. "I wish the sausage was off

my nose . . . and in the frying pan!"

And – *pfff!* – the sausage jumped off his nose, and there it was in the frying-pan, going *sizzle-sizzle*!

"So, that's the three wishes gone," said Jack. "But we do have a big fat sausage for supper and not CABBAGE SOUP!"

Then Jack and Mary sat down and shared the sausage. And it was the juiciest, yummiest sausage they had ever tasted. Of course, it had to be! It was a magic sausage! And they are the best.

So now, when you meet a woodland elf, and – *pfff!* – he gives you three magic wishes, think carefully before you decide what you would like to have.

Anna
and the Shaggy Bear

ONCE UPON A TIME, there was a little girl called Anna who lived with her grandma and grandpa and a big bouncy dog in a cottage beside a forest.

One morning Anna's friends knocked at the door and asked her to come and pick wild strawberries in the forest. But her grandma said, "No, you can't go. You're only little. You might get lost."

ANNA AND THE SHAGGY BEAR

Anna wanted to go so much that she kept asking, on and on, until Grandma said, "All right. But you must keep close to the paths and stay with your friends."

Quickly, before Grandma changed her mind, Anna tied a red flowery scarf under her chin, picked up Grandma's basket, and skipped off with her friends.

At first, Anna was careful. She kept close to the paths and stayed with her friends. But, after a while, she saw some strawberries in among the trees, and she skipped over and picked them.

When her basket was almost full, she looked around. But she couldn't see her friends. She listened. But she couldn't hear them. She called, "WHERE ARE YOU?" But they didn't answer. So she walked back the way she thought she had come. But there were trees everywhere, and she didn't find the path. And though she called and called, she didn't find her friends.

After a while, evening came and it grew dark, so Anna decided to climb a tree. "In the morning," she said, "Grandma and Grandpa and our big bouncy dog will come looking, and they will find me."

She put her basket on the ground and climbed a tall tree

and sat down on a strong branch. She tried to be brave, but she was cold and hungry, and she began to cry.

Presently a shaggy bear came trotting by. He heard Anna crying and looked up. "Little girl," he said, "what's the matter?"

"I'm lost," said Anna. "I don't know the way home."

"Come down, little girl," said the bear. "I'll carry you to my house, and tomorrow I'll take you home."

He spoke so kindly that Anna climbed down. The bear bent low and Anna jumped on his back. He picked up the basket of strawberries and trotted off to his house, deep in the forest.

The next day Anna and the bear had strawberries for breakfast. When they had finished, Anna said, "Now, please, Shaggy Bear, take me home."

"I'm too busy today," said the bear. "So be a good

little girl and light the stove and cook some porridge for our dinner."

Then the bear trotted off into the forest. And Anna lit the stove and cooked some porridge.

The next morning, Anna said, "Please, Shaggy Bear, take me home."

But the bear said, "No, I won't! I want you to stay

here always and light the stove and cook my dinner!"

Anna kept asking, on and on. But every time the bear just said "NO – I – WON'T!".

One morning, Anna said, "If you won't take me back to my grandma and grandpa, I shall bake some cherry pies and put them in a basket. Then you must take them to their cottage and leave them on the doorstep, so they'll know I am alive and well."

"All right," said the bear. "I'll do that."

"You must keep your promise, Shaggy Bear," said Anna, "because I'll be watching you. I shall climb to the tip-top of the cherry tree in your garden and keep my eyes on you every step of the way."

As soon as the bear trotted off into the forest, Anna picked some cherries and made some pies. When they were all baked and ready, she wrapped them in her red flowery scarf. And then – guess what she did –

she climbed into Grandma's basket, curled up small and covered herself with the red flowery scarf that was full of cherry pies.

When the bear came back and saw the basket, he prowled around. *Sniff! sniff! sniff!* "Something smells good," he said, and bent down to look inside.

But a loud voice said, "Shaggy Bear! Don't touch! Those pies are for my grandma and grandpa, and nobody else in the world. Pick up the basket, Shaggy Bear, and off you go!"

"My! Oh my!" growled the bear. "That little girl has got eyes everywhere. Best do what she says."

So he picked up the basket and trotted off, towards Anna's cottage.

When he was halfway there, he sat down. "Time to taste one of those cherry pies," he said.

But a loud voice said, "Shaggy Bear! Don't touch!

Those pies are for my grandma and grandpa, and nobody else in the world. Up you get, Shaggy Bear, and off you go!"

"My! Oh my!" he growled. "That little girl has got eyes everywhere."

He picked up the basket and trotted off, until he came to the door of Anna's cottage. Then he put the basket down. "Now I'll taste one of those pies," he said.

But a loud voice said, "Shaggy Bear! Don't touch! Those pies are for my grandma and grandpa, and nobody

else in the world. Off you go, Shaggy Bear! Back to your own house!"

"Don't care who they're for!" growled the bear. "I'm hungry!"

He reached out a paw. He touched the red flowery scarf. But the next moment, a big bouncy dog bounded round the corner of the cottage – *slap-bang!* – into the bear and knocked him over. *"Wuff! wuff!"* barked the dog. *"Wuff! wuff! wuff!"*

The bear didn't know who this big bouncy creature

was that had *slap-bang*ed into him. And he didn't stop to find out. He trotted off, back to the forest, growling, "My! Oh my! That little girl has got eyes everywhere! My! Oh my!" And Anna never saw that shaggy bear ever again!

Well, next thing, the cottage door opened and there stood Anna's grandma and grandpa. Then Anna climbed out of the basket, and in her hands she held the red flowery scarf, full of cherry pies.

"Look! I've brought you a present," she said.

And you can guess what happened next. Lots of hugs! Lots

of kisses! And the big bouncy dog joined in. He gave Anna licky kisses all over. Then they went into the cottage and ate cherry pies. Grandpa ate three, Grandma ate two, and Anna was so happy and excited that she could only manage one. But the big bouncy dog made up for her. He ate six, because those cherry pies that Anna had made tasted really, truly delicious.

Twenty Cheeky
Monkeys

ONCE THERE WAS A SMALL GIRL who loved wearing hats. Red, green and yellow. Blue and purple. Stripy hats. Zig-zaggy patterned hats. Embroidered hats. Any kind of hat. She just loved putting a hat on her head. It made her feel grand and grown-up.

The girl, whose name was Ngozi, was lucky, because her mother made hats. So there were always lots of beautiful hats at home to try on.

Every few weeks, Ngozi's mother piled the hats she had made into a basket, and swung it up on top of her head. Ngozi tied her baby brother on to her mother's back. And then off they walked, along the path, through the jungly forest, till they came to the market where they sold the hats.

But one time, when market day came round, Ngozi's baby brother was sick, and her mother decided to stay at home and look after him. "I want you to take the hats to market and sell them," she said. "Can you do that?"

"Oh, yes!" said Ngozi.

"There are twenty-one hats. Now, don't lose any!"

"Oh, no!" said Ngozi.

Then her mother piled the twenty-one hats into the basket. Ngozi swung it up on top of her head, and off she walked along the path through the jungly forest.

But Ngozi's baby brother had kept her awake most

of the night with his crying, and she soon felt tired. So when she came to a clearing in the jungly forest, she put her basket on the ground and sat down. She reached over and chose her favourite hat: a red, yellow and green one, with a black-and-white zig-zaggy pattern. She put the hat on her head, rested her back against a tree, closed her eyes and fell asleep.

After a while Ngozi woke. She rubbed her sleepy eyes, stretched and stood up. She reached over to the basket . . . but there were no hats inside. It was empty!

Ngozi looked on the grass. No hats. She looked up – and what did she see?

A whole troop of monkeys sitting in the trees . . . and every monkey had a HAT on its head. Just like Ngozi.

Then she knew what had happened. Those cheeky monkeys had crept down while she was sleeping. Every one had chosen a hat, put it on and climbed back up again.

Ngozi was so upset, she shook a fist at them and shouted, "Give me back my hats!"

But all the monkeys just shook a fist and shouted back, *"Jibba! jibba! jibba!"*

Ngozi stamped her feet and shouted, "Give me back my hats!"

And all the monkeys jumped up and down on the branches and shouted, *"Jibba! jibba! jibba!"*

Then Ngozi had a thought. Maybe the monkeys didn't understand.

So Ngozi patted her hat. Then she shouted, very loud

indeed, "Give me back my hats!"

But it was no use. The monkeys just patted their hats and shouted, *"Jibba! jibba! jibba!"*

Now, what could she do? She had lost twenty hats. What would her mother say?

Ngozi was so very upset, she snatched her hat off her head and flung it on the ground.

Then twenty monkeys snatched their hats off their heads. Just like Ngozi.

Twenty hats came flying through the air and landed on the ground!

Quick! quick! Ngozi picked up

the hats and piled them into the basket.

"Goodbye, you cheeky monkeys!" she called, and gave them a wave.

The twenty cheeky monkeys shouted, *"Jibba! jibba! jibba!"*

And they waved. Just like Ngozi.

Quick! quick! Ngozi hurried off to the market. And, do you know, she sold every hat in the basket.

Twenty-one hats!

She was so happy, she smiled all the way home.

And when she got there, her baby brother was well again – and he was smiling.

Ngozi's mother was smiling too. "Well done, Ngozi. You sold every hat!" she said. "You didn't lose any! I am so pleased, I'm going to make an extra-special hat. Just for you. Choose your favourite colours."

Ngozi chose red, yellow and green.

"And can you put a black-and-white zig-zaggy pattern on it?" she asked.

"Of course I can," said her mother.

When the extra-special hat was ready, Ngozi put it on her head. Then she walked about, nose in the air, and she felt extra-specially grand and grown-up.

Little Red Hen
and the Rascally Fox

ONCE UPON A TIME, Little Red Hen lived by herself in a little house with a lovely garden all around. Over the hill, in a dark den among the rocks, lived a rascally fox and an old mother fox.

This rascally fox thought Little Red Hen would make a very tasty dinner, so he kept trying to catch her.

But Little Red Hen was too clever for him. Every time she left home, she locked the door behind her, and every time she came back, she locked the door behind her and put the key in her apron pocket where she kept her scissors, needle and thread, and a piece of sugar candy.

At last, one night when he was lying in bed, the rascally fox worked out a way to catch Little Red Hen.

Early the next morning, he said to the old mother fox, "When I come home, have the pan on the fire, with the

water boiling, because today, for sure, I shall bring back Little Red Hen!"

He slung a bag over his shoulder, and away he ran, until he came to Little Red Hen's garden. Then he crept in and hid behind some bushes.

After a while, Little Red Hen opened the door. She looked about, but she couldn't see anyone. So she stepped over to the wood pile and quickly picked up some sticks for her fire.

As soon as her back was turned, the rascally fox slipped into the house and hid behind the door.

A few moments later, Little Red Hen hurried back in. She dropped the sticks and closed the door. She was just going to lock it when she heard – *swish swish swish!* And then she saw the rascally fox, with the bag slung over his shoulder, and his long bushy tail spread out behind, going *swish swish swish*!

Little Red Hen was scared. But – *whoooosh!* – she flew straight up to the wooden beam near the ceiling and perched there.

"Ah-ha! You may as well go home," she said. "You can't and you won't catch me, you rascally fox!"

"Ah-ha! Can't I?" said the rascally fox.

And he began to whirl round and round in a circle, chasing his own tail. Faster, faster, faster he whirled until poor Little Red Hen got so dizzy with watching that . . .

Plop! – she dropped off the beam and landed in the middle of the floor.

Then the rascally fox picked her up, stuffed her in the bag, slung the bag over his shoulder, opened the door, and away he ran.

Poor Little Red Hen was all smothered and hot inside the bag. So she took her scissors out of her pocket and – *snip! snip!* – she cut a hole in the bag, stuck her head out and looked around.

Now, with all the running and whirling, the rascally fox began to feel tired, so he stopped for a rest. And the next thing, he began to snore. *Hunch-chrrr! Hunch-chrr!*

Then – *snip! snip! snip!* – Little Red Hen cut the hole bigger and jumped out. She found a big stone and pushed it into the bag. She took out her needle and thread, and quickly stitched up the hole. Then she ran home, as fast as she could.

When she got home, she locked the door behind her. "Ah-ha!" she chuckled. "You couldn't and you didn't catch me, you rascally fox!" And then she ate a piece of her favourite sugar candy.

Now, as soon as he woke, the rascally fox was off, carrying the bag, the same as before. When he came to his dark den among the rocks, he said to the old mother fox, "Have you the pan on the fire? And is the water boiling?"

"The water is bubbling and steaming," she said. "But have you got Little Red Hen?"

"I have! She's in the bag," he said. "Now let's boil her up for our dinner!"

The old mother fox took the lid off the pan. The rascally fox lifted the bag, gave it a shake and out fell – A BIG STONE!

"*Huhhh!*" growled the rascally fox. "Little Red Hen is too clever for me. I won't EVER visit her house again."

And he didn't.

So Little Red Hen lived happily ever after, in her own little house with the lovely garden all around.

The Enormous
Turnip

THERE WAS ONCE A LITTLE OLD MAN who worked all year round growing vegetables to feed himself and his wife.

One spring day he planted some turnip seeds. He covered them over with soil and watered them well. "Grow, little seeds, grow," he said.

The Enormous Turnip

And they did. Tiny green shoots peeped up through the soil, and soon the plants grew up, strong and sturdy.

But one turnip grew faster than the rest. First it was twice the size of the others, then four times bigger, then eight times bigger, and it kept on growing.

One day, the old man's wife said to him, "Why don't you pull up that enormous turnip, so we can have turnip stew for supper?"

So the little old man went out into the garden. He grasped the enormous turnip and pulled. He pulled and pulled. But the turnip didn't budge.

So the little old man shouted to his wife. The little old woman pulled the little old man, and the little old man pulled the turnip.

They pulled and pulled. But the turnip didn't budge.

So the little old woman went next door to fetch the little girl.

The little girl pulled the little old woman, the little old woman pulled the little old man, and the little old man pulled the turnip. They pulled and pulled. But the turnip didn't budge.

So the little girl ran to fetch her brother.

The little boy pulled the little girl, the little girl pulled the little old woman, the little old woman pulled the little old man, and the little old man pulled the turnip. They pulled and pulled. But the turnip didn't budge.

So the little boy whistled for his dog.

The dog pulled the little boy, the little boy pulled the little girl, the little girl pulled the little old woman, the little old woman pulled the little old man, and the little old man pulled the turnip. They pulled and pulled.

But the turnip didn't budge.

So the dog barked for the cat.

The cat pulled the dog, the dog pulled the little boy, the little boy pulled the little girl, the little girl pulled the little old woman, the little old woman pulled the little old man, and the little old man pulled the turnip. They pulled and pulled. But the turnip still didn't budge.

So the cat mewed for the mouse.

The mouse pulled the cat, the cat pulled the dog, the dog pulled the little boy, the little boy pulled the little girl, the little girl pulled the little old woman, the little old woman pulled the little old man, and the little old man pulled the turnip.

They pulled and pulled and *pulled*.

And – *whoosh!* – up came the enormous turnip!

The little old woman cooked the enormous turnip in an enormous pot, and the enormous stew was enough to feed everyone: the mouse, the cat, the dog, the little boy, the little girl, the little old woman and the little old man. They had never eaten a tastier meal in their lives.

The Town Mouse
and the Country Mouse

THERE WAS ONCE A COUNTRY MOUSE who lived in a little house under the hedgerow. Every day he swept his house clean and went out into the fields to find seeds and nuts and fruits for his larder. His life was simple, but he was happy, for he had everything he needed.

One day, a visitor came to the little house under the hedgerow. It was Country Mouse's cousin, Town Mouse.

She lived in the big city. Country Mouse made her a bed of sweet-smelling hay and gathered the plumpest nuts, grains and berries for her to eat. He was sure she would enjoy herself in the country.

But at suppertime, Town Mouse frowned. "Dear Cousin, is this all you eat? Nuts and berries? I live in a fine, big house where there is as much food as I want, and no need to go

out and gather it. You should come to stay with me."

After supper, Country Mouse showed Town Mouse the bed he had prepared for her.

But Town Mouse frowned. "I shan't sleep a wink on that bundle of hay. At home, I have a soft feather bed. You should come and try it, Cousin."

Country Mouse couldn't sleep for a long time that night. He kept thinking about the fine, big house where Town Mouse lived, and her soft feather bed. How wonderful it sounded.

In the morning, Country Mouse took Town Mouse for a walk in the cornfield. Town Mouse complained as the corn stalks scratched her. Then a weasel ran by and scared her so much that she jumped.

"What a horrible creature!" cried Town Mouse. "Oh, Cousin, I don't like the country. I'm going home tomorrow. Why don't you come with me? You'll see how much nicer it is to live in the town."

Country Mouse agreed. He wanted to see his cousin's fine, big house, and sleep in her soft feather bed.

So the next day, the two mice set off for the town.

It was almost dark when they arrived. Country Mouse's eyes were dazzled by the bright lights. He kept close to his cousin, scared by the loud noises and the heavy tramp of feet as people walked past.

Finally they arrived at Town Mouse's house.

Country Mouse felt better at once. It was as big and as fine as his cousin had described.

"This way," said Town Mouse, disappearing into a hole in the wall.

First they came to the kitchen. Laid out on the table were all kinds of wonderful things to eat: bread and butter, fruit cake, a block of delicious cheese, a bowl of bright red strawberries and a jug of cream.

"You see, Cousin! There's as much food as you can eat!" said Town Mouse.

But Country Mouse had barely eaten a mouthful when the door burst open and in walked the cook.

"Quick!" whispered Town Mouse. "Hide!"

Town Mouse crept behind the jug of cream and Country Mouse followed.

There they stayed while the cook rolled pastry to make a pie.

As soon as she left the kitchen, the two mice slipped from their hiding place and started to nibble.

But not for long.

There, in front of the fireplace, licking its lips, was an enormous cat.

Country Mouse was scared. The cat was looking straight at him. Oh, how he wished he were safely back in the country!

"Quick, Cousin! Over here!"

Town Mouse had leapt from the table and was racing across the floor. Country Mouse followed then – *zippety-zip* – he dived through a gap in the floorboards just as the hungry cat pounced.

That night, Country Mouse curled up on Town Mouse's feather bed. It was just as soft as his cousin had said, but he could not sleep.

Not a wink. Not while a hungry cat waited outside the mousehole!

"It was kind of you to show me your home, but I really must go," he said to Town Mouse the next morning.

"You can't leave without breakfast," said Town Mouse. "Besides, there's so much you still need to see!"

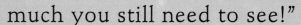

"I've seen quite enough, thank you, Cousin" said Country Mouse.

Wishing Town Mouse goodbye, he hurried back to the hole in the wall, ran through the town and didn't stop till he was all the way home.

And from that day on, Country Mouse never left his little house under the hedgerow. He never dreamt of fine, big houses or soft feather beds again.

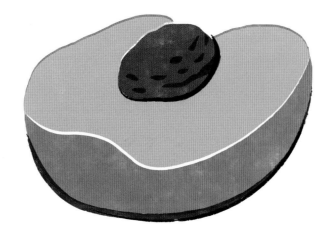

Little Peachling
and the Giants

ONCE UPON A TIME, there lived a poor old man and a poor old woman who were very sad because they had no children.

One day, the old woman decided to do some washing, so she piled the dirty clothes into a basket, and off she went down to the river. There she *slish-slosh*ed and *rub-rub-rubb*ed until the clothes were clean.

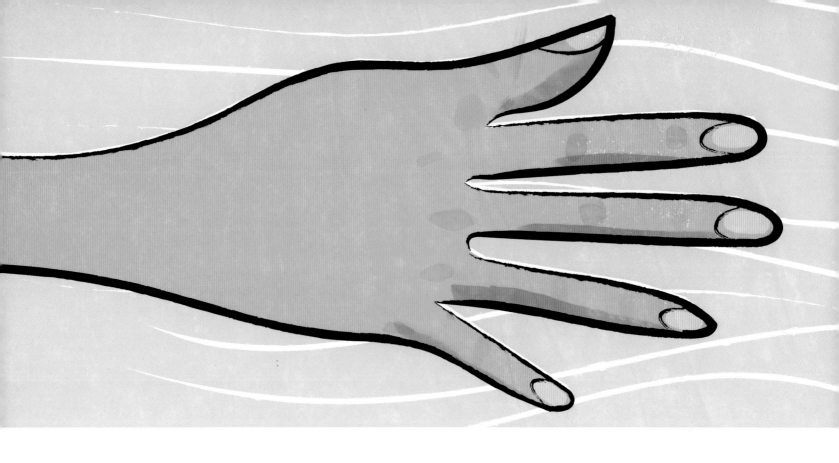

She had just piled everything back into the basket, when she saw something floating down the river. It was a big, rosy red peach. It floated closer. The old woman reached out and it floated right into her hands.

"This is my good-luck day!" she said. And she tucked the peach in among the clothes, picked up the basket and hurried home.

As soon as she saw the old man, she called out, "Look what I found in the river!"

"What a big, rosy red peach!" said the old man. "Let's cut it up and eat it."

But the next moment, the peach burst open – and inside it was a little baby boy.

"Ohhh! At last we have a baby of our own!" exclaimed the old woman. "What shall we call him?"

"We'll call him Little Peachling," said the old man. "Because we found him in a peach, and he is very little."

And that was the name they gave him.

Well, Little Peachling was a hungry baby. He ate one half of the peach – he ate the other half – and he grew. He ate a bowl of rice and a bowl of fish, and he grew and grew. Never has a baby eaten so much or grown so fast.

Soon he could walk and talk, and before long he was a tall, strong boy. The old man and the old woman loved him very much. And he loved them back, and always called them Grandfather and Grandmother, because they were old.

Now, not far off, in a castle by the sea, lived some wicked giants. They were forever stomping out of their castle and stealing money, jewels, and any treasures they could find. Everyone was afraid of them.

One day, Little Peachling bowed his head and said most politely, "Grandfather, Grandmother, I must go to the giants' castle and stop their wickedness."

The old man shook his head slowly and said:

"The giants are tough and they're wicked too!
You'd better take care or they might kill you!"

But Little Peachling said, "I'm not scared of them!"

"Little Peachling!" cried the old woman. "Bravest Boy! Number One Hero!"

Then she gave him new trousers and tied a scarf about his head. She cooked some rice cakes and put them in a bag and hung it from his belt. And then he was ready.

"Goodbye! Goodbye!" he called as he jogged off.

"Good luck!" they called after him.

Little Peachling hadn't gone far when a big yellow dog came running from among the tall grass. *"Woo-oof!* I am Fiercest Dog," he barked.

"Where are you going?"

"To the giants' castle!" said Little Peachling.

Fiercest Dog said:

"The giants are tough and they're wicked too!

But give me a rice cake, and I'll come with you!"

So Little Peachling gave him a rice cake, and they jogged off.

They hadn't gone far when a red-capped pheasant flew down. *"Ken-ken!* I am Strongest Pheasant," he screeched. "Where are you going?"

"To the giants' castle," said Little Peachling.

Strongest Pheasant said:

"The giants are tough and they're wicked too!

But give me a rice cake, and I'll come with you!"

So Little Peachling gave him a rice cake. Strongest Pheasant perched on his shoulder, and they all jogged off.

They hadn't gone far when a grey monkey swung down from a tree.

"*Kia-kia!* I am Cleverest Monkey," he chattered. "Where are you going?"

"To the giants' castle," said Little Peachling.

Cleverest Monkey said:

"*The giants are tough and they're wicked too!*

But give me a rice cake, and I'll come with you!"

So Little Peachling gave him a rice cake. Cleverest Monkey jumped on Fiercest Dog's back, and they all jogged off.

At last they came to a huge castle by the sea. There was a wall around it and a gate, all bolted and barred. How could they get in?

Well, Strongest Pheasant flew over the wall. Cleverest Monkey climbed over the gate, pulled back the bolts and bars, and opened it. Then Fiercest Dog and Little Peachling jogged in.

But, next thing, lots of giants came stomping out of the castle. They were HUGE, and they looked TOUGH and FIERCE.

But Little Peachling sang out:

"You may be tough and wicked too –

But we're Number One Heroes and not scared of you!"

Then the fight began. Fiercest Dog bit the giants' ankles. Strongest Pheasant pecked their noses. Cleverest Monkey tugged their hair and pinched them. And Little Peachling wrestled. He tossed a giant – *wheee!* – to one side. He tossed another giant – *wheee!* – up in the air. And – *wheee! wheee!* – he kept on tossing.

Those giants were scared. They ran helter-skelter back into the castle and hid. Only the king of the giants remained.

"Please, don't hurt us," he said. "We'll give you our treasure! As much as you want!"

"All right," said Little Peachling. "Give us a great cartload of treasure, and promise there will be no more stealing, no more wickedness."

"I promise," said the king of the giants. "We will stop being wicked. We will!" He called the other giants, and they came creeping out of the castle. They quickly found a cart and piled it high with treasure – gold, silver, jade, all sorts of jewels – so much treasure!

Then the heroes were off. Little Peachling and Fiercest Dog led the way. Cleverest Monkey sat on top of the

treasure, while Strongest Pheasant pulled the cart, and the wheels went round, *kirro! kirro!*

When Little Peachling came to his own home, he sang out:

"We've beaten the giants and scared them too!

They never again will steal from you!"

"Little Peachling!" cried the old woman. "Bravest Boy! Number One Hero!"

But Little Peachling said, "Grandmother, here are three other Number One Heroes: Fiercest Dog, Strongest Pheasant and Cleverest Monkey! Without their help, I could not have beaten the giants!"

Then off went the three helpers. Their work was done.

"Goodbye, Little Peachling!" they called. "Goodbye!"

And did those giants keep their promise?

Yes, they did. They stopped doing wicked things.

So from then on, the old man and the old woman lived in peace. They had plenty of everything. But, best of all, they had their son – Little Peachling.

The Elves and the
Shoemaker

THERE WAS ONCE A SHOEMAKER who lived in a great city. He and his wife worked hard, but business was bad. They were so poor that one day they had no money to buy food for their supper.

The shoemaker had just enough leather for one pair of shoes. That night, he cut out the leather with care, and laid the pieces on his workbench to sew the next day. Then he and his wife went to bed.

In the morning, the shoemaker went straight to work – but the pieces of leather were gone.

In their place was a pair of new shoes. The stitches were exquisitely tiny and neat, the leather polished and glowing.

"Who could have done this?" the shoemaker marvelled. He had never seen a more beautiful pair of shoes.

Just then, a gentleman walked into the shop. "What a wonderful pair of shoes. I have never seen finer. I'll buy them."

And he handed the shoemaker a golden coin.

The coin bought a fish for supper and enough leather for two more pairs of shoes.

That night, the shoemaker cut out the leather. He

laid the pieces on his workbench, and then he went to bed.

In the morning, there were two pairs of beautiful shoes on the workbench, made with the same tiny stitches.

The shoemaker sold them at once. He bought a chicken for supper and enough leather for four pairs of shoes.

That night, he cut out the leather, and then he went to bed.

And in the morning, four pairs of beautiful shoes were standing on the workbench.

So it was for many weeks.

Leather was bought.

THE ELVES AND THE SHOEMAKER

Pieces were cut.

Beautiful shoes appeared, all made with the same tiny stitches.

The shoemaker and his wife were no longer poor. "We must find out who is making these shoes and thank them," the shoemaker said to his wife.

So instead of going to bed that night, they hid in a corner of the workroom. They waited and waited. Then, as the clock struck midnight, who should run in but two tiny elves!

They scrambled up on to the workbench. *Tap! tap! tap!* went their hammers. *Flash!* went their needles as they sewed at lightning speed. Soon a row of beautiful shoes appeared. Then the elves jumped down from the workbench and ran out of the door.

And the funniest thing? They weren't wearing a stitch of clothing!

The shoemaker and his wife looked at each other. How could they thank those two tiny elves?

"I have an idea," said the shoemaker's wife. "They must be cold without clothes. I'll make them each an outfit and a thick, warm coat, and I'll knit them socks and tights."

"And I'll make them shoes from the softest leather," said the shoemaker. "We'll do it tomorrow."

The next night, everything was ready. The shoemaker and his wife laid the clothes and shoes on the workbench, then hid in the corner to wait.

The clock struck midnight.

In ran the elves.

When they saw the clothes and shoes, they clapped

their hands and quickly put them on. They were so pleased! And then? They danced around the room and out of the door, and that was the last that the shoemaker and his wife ever saw of them.

But the shoemaker always had work, for the shoes he made were almost – *almost!* – as beautiful as those made by the two tiny elves.

The End